Murder in the Open Air

A Little Firling Mystery – Book Seven

by Belinda Chavremootoo

Dedication

For every cat who ever solved a mystery quietly before the humans caught up. Especially one.

Text Copyright

Coming Soon: Murder in the Tides

A Little Firling Mystery – Book Eight

A drifting body.

A misdirection in the water.

And a murder that was never meant to reach the shore.

When Annabel, Evie, and Persephone discover the woman face down in the reeds, they expect answers to follow.

But no one knows her.

No one reported her missing.

And the water in her lungs... doesn't belong to the river.

The tides have carried more than just secrets.

They've brought death.

Table of Contents

Prologue

Twenty Years Ago

Briarley Estate, Summer Night

The first time the play was staged at Briarley, the roses bloomed late and the storm came early.

The lawn had been set for a dream — velvet drapes hung between the trees, paper lanterns bobbed from the orchard branches, and someone had even scattered wildflower petals along the makeshift aisles. It was meant to be a gift. A celebration. A night of lightness and laughter before everything changed.

But nothing stayed light for long.

Not here.

Not in Firling.

***

Backstage — though no one called it that then — a girl stood in the half-shadow of the garden wall; her costume torn slightly at the sleeve. She pressed her script against her chest like it could steady her heartbeat.

From the orchard path, someone else was running. Late. Breathless.

Whispers rose like smoke. Accusations. Regrets.

The audience clapped once — twice — then fell silent.

Something had gone wrong.

Not loudly.

But enough.

***

Later, when the lanterns had burned low and the thunder had passed, there were questions.

About what had been said offstage.

About who had left early, and who never left at all.

About why the play had never been performed again.

Until now.

Chapter 1

The gardens at Briarley Estate were in bloom. Roses curled over trellises in defiant blush, lavender buzzed with bees like gossip on wings, and hollyhocks loomed tall as if judging everything below. The air smelled of paint, petals, and anticipation — the kind that clung to skin even more stubbornly than heat.

Annabel Lennox Deighton adjusted her sunhat and watched from the edge of the lawn, notebook in hand, her usual seat of quiet observation. It had been just over a year since she arrived in Little Firling. Long enough to know who put cream or jam first on their scones. Long enough to be invited to things without suspicion. But not quite long enough to stop asking the kinds of questions other people avoided.

Especially today.

A *Midsummer Night's Dream* — open-air, full-cast, professionally lit, and slightly too ambitious for a village of 800.

It was the first time a play had been staged on the Briarley Estate grounds in over two decades.

No one really said why.

***

She scanned the cast as they arrived. The familiar figures didn't need introduction. Clarissa Fairmont, former opera soprano and self-appointed drama queen, swept onto the grass as if summoned by thunder. Jasper Wyatt, from the bakery, carried three clipboards and a face full of earnest nerves. Bettany Marlowe was already near the costume rail, silent as ever, mending something long before it had time to tear. Kitty Simmons sat beneath the mulberry tree, notebook open, gaze flicking away from the lawn too often to be accidental.

But it wasn't the locals that made Annabel pause.

It was the *others*.

They hadn't been in Firling last spring. Or winter. Or ever, as far as anyone could remember. And yet here they were — sprinkled through the cast and crew, all with polite smiles and vague explanations.

Olivia Vale, playing Helena, had arrived with three matching suitcases and the kind of London enunciation that made village dogs bark. Victor Lang said he was from Theo Harper's old technical team, but he'd asked Bernard Harper about the estate's *foundations.* Delphine Ray claimed to be an old friend of Juliet Hayes' — though Juliet, notably, hadn't introduced her. And Leo Marks? He was too charming, too quiet, and took too many notes that didn't seem to have anything to do with blocking.

They were here for the play.

Supposedly.

But Annabel had taught enough tragedy to recognize a cast that wasn't saying all their lines out loud.

***

At the centre of it all stood Theo Harper. London theatre director. Local returnee. And very much the man of the moment.

He wore sunglasses too dark for the weather, a scarf too long for July, and a smile that never quite reached his eyes.

"Annabel, darling," he called, striding toward her with arms outstretched.

"Isn't it *divine?* It's exactly as I imagined it."

"Which part?" she asked, adjusting her pen. "The wild roses or the existential dread?"

Theo laughed too hard. "Oh, I've missed your wit."

"You haven't been gone long enough to miss anything," she said flatly.

He waved her off. "Art takes us places, darling. Besides, this play — it's not just nostalgia. It's the beginning of something. The world's watching more than you think."

That was what unsettled her.

The quiet hum of something larger.

Not just a play. Not just Firling.

Something else was unfolding here — something stitched between the lines of Shakespeare and the shade of the old estate trees. Something moneyed. Carefully positioned. Maybe even filmed.

She'd overheard one of the newcomers ask if the back lawn had "soundproofing."

What kind of village theatre needed *soundproofing?*

***

Evie arrived beside her, clipboard in hand, oversized sunglasses on, and a straw poking out of a suspiciously pink thermos.

"Theo's rewritten Oberon's entrance again," she muttered. "Clarissa's threatening to stage a revolt. And someone's painted Titania's throne in mauve. *Mauve*, Annabel. We're two arguments away from a Shakespearean cage match."

"And yet," Annabel said, eyes scanning the lawn again, "something tells me this won't be the worst part of the production."

Persephone padded up the path and curled herself beside a crate of fake ivy. She blinked once. Slowly.

Someone offstage whispered a line that wasn't in the play:

"Not all fairies bring wonder. Some bring warning."

Annabel turned her head sharply.

No one was there.

Not yet.

Chapter 2

The moment Titania's entrance was announced for Scene Two, Clarissa Fairmont swept onto the lawn with the subtlety of a stagecoach on fire.

"What," she thundered, "has happened to my crown?"

Everyone froze.

The crown — a delicately crafted circlet of gold ivy, glinting beads, and what Clarissa had described as *"emotional truth in accessory form"* — was not on the costume rail where she had allegedly left it.

"I placed it right *here*," she declared, pointing to a nondescript patch of grass, "beside that tragic pile of faux greenery. And now it's vanished. *Vanished.* Which, incidentally, is what happened to the dignity of theatre when people started casting influencers—"

Theo clapped once, sharp and theatrical. "People, please. Props move. Lives evolve. We mustn't be derailed by a crown."

Clarissa turned slowly; eyebrow raised like a guillotine.

"You want me to embody a faerie queen without her crown?" she asked, voice trembling with righteous outrage. "That's like asking Prospero to conjure without his staff. Or asking me to deliver passion while dressed in this *shade* of mauve."

"You *chose* that shade," someone muttered near the sound table.

Clarissa ignored them. She pivoted dramatically to Annabel.

"Professor Deighton. What does Shakespeare say about artistic sabotage?"

Annabel didn't look up from her notes. "That it comes before a fall."

Clarissa huffed. "Quoting Proverbs in the midst of a rehearsal. We are truly in decline."

***

Evie appeared beside Annabel, clipboard in one hand, wine gums in the other.

"Two silver pieces. I say that the crown will turn up on top of her own mirror later," she whispered.

"I'm not taking that bet," Annabel replied.

Persephone trotted onto the lawn, tail raised like an exclamation point, and began a slow, investigative circle around the prop bench.

Then she stopped, her whole-body stiff.

A second later, she hissed and jumped back.

Annabel stood immediately. "Persephone?"

Evie turned. "That sounded... pointy."

They moved toward the source of the hiss: an overturned crate full of faux ivy and old costume bits. Among the disarray was a half-open envelope — yellowing, curled at the edges, and carrying a scent so thick it almost felt visible.

Annabel picked it up carefully.

It smelled like old theatre dressing rooms — heady florals, powder, and a hint of something sharp. A perfume that no one wore anymore. Or shouldn't.

Evie leaned in. "That's not perfume. That's... an ancestor."

Inside the envelope was nothing but a single dried violet. Pressed flat. Preserved intentionally.

On the front, one word was scrawled in elegant, faded handwriting:

Hannah.

***

Later, while the faeries argued over where to stand and Puck accidentally tripped over a fallen lantern, Annabel sat with Bettany Marlowe beneath the edge of the orchard.

Bettany's fingers worked a needle through a hem, her motions smooth and practiced. She hadn't spoken during the earlier commotion. She never really did.

"You know this isn't the first time they staged a play here," she said softly.

Annabel looked over. "I heard that."

"There's a reason no one talks about it."

Bettany tied off the thread. Her eyes stayed on the fabric.

"It didn't end well."

Annabel tilted her head. "Were you—"

But Bettany stood before she could finish. Quietly. Gracefully. And left the hem unfinished.

***

The kitchen of the Honeystone Cottage was warm with rosemary and roasting courgettes that evening. Annabel moved between oven and counter like someone solving a riddle through ingredients. She cooked when she needed to think. Always had.

Evie leaned against the butcher's block, attempting to slice tomatoes without maiming them.

"I still say the crown thing was deliberate," she said. "Clarissa thrives on minor chaos. She's like a peony with teeth."

Annabel stirred the vegetables. "She was more theatrical than usual."

"She compared herself to Oberon and Elizabeth I *in the same breath.*"

"That's not unusual for her."

"No, but Victor's reaction was," Evie said. "Did you see him during the scene? He wasn't watching Clarissa. He was watching *Theo.*"

Annabel didn't reply. She reached for her notebook, opened it on the table, and slid out the envelope they'd found.

"Still can't stop thinking about this?" Evie asked, joining her.

Annabel nodded. "The perfume. The dried flower. The handwriting."

"And the name. Hannah." Evie frowned. "We don't know a Hannah, do we?"

"Not that I recall."

Persephone hopped up onto the dresser, blinked once, and stretched herself into a long curl of feline scepticism.

Annabel turned the envelope over in her hands. "It doesn't make sense to leave something like this in a prop crate. It feels intentional. Like someone wanted it to be found."

"Or someone wanted to remind someone else."

They ate in silence for a while, the wine cool against the warmth of the room.

Outside, the village was still, except for the occasional sound of late laughter drifting from the road — just a little too loud for how quiet the night felt.

"You know," Evie said, "some of the cast members aren't acting. Not really."

Annabel looked up.

"They watched today like it was more than a rehearsal," Evie continued. "Like they were waiting to see if something would happen."

Annabel didn't smile.

"Like they were studying a *scene.*"

Chapter 3

The moment Annabel stepped outside; she could feel it — the village had begun to hum.

Not in the bright, cheery way it did before fêtes or spring fairs. This was the low, persistent buzz of curiosity fermenting.

Outside the post office, Ronnie Parkes was adjusting his bicycle chain while simultaneously talking to no one in particular.

"I'm not saying they're up to something," he muttered, loud enough to be overheard, "but when one of them asks if the estate has any underground chambers, you start wondering if we've accidentally cast a spy thriller."

He looked up as Annabel approached, grinning. "Morning, Professor. You surviving the theatricals?"

"So far," she said. "Though the script might not."

"Word is someone rewrote a scene to include dry ice and a power ballad."

He leaned closer. "And I'm not saying who, but it rhymes with *Barissa*."

***

The walk through the village was a parade of sideways glances and polite disapproval dressed up as small talk.

Outside the bakery, Mrs. Gilchrist was debating whether Olivia Vale's voice was "naturally that posh" or just for show. Someone at the grocer's had apparently sold six bottles of elderflower gin in three days — rehearsal stress, no doubt.

But it wasn't until Annabel stepped into the Hare & Hound that the true pulse of Little Firling made itself known.

***

It was mid-morning, but already three regulars sat by the fireplace nursing tea with the quiet intensity of men preparing to critique a performance they had no intention of attending.

At the bar, Henry Griggs, the bartender, was setting out a fresh pot of coffee. Bernard Harper, as usual, was polishing a glass that probably didn't need it.

"Morning," Annabel said.

"Back for round two?" Bernard asked.

"I thought I might have some tea before someone else delivers a monologue."

Henry poured without asking.

Across the room, Celia Ward of the WI was leaning conspiratorially across a table, speaking just loudly enough to be overheard.

"They say it's different this time," she was saying. "More professional. More polished. But I remember the last time we had theatre at Briarley. I remember the way it *ended*."

One of the others at her table leaned in. "Didn't someone fall off the stage?"

Celia sniffed. "No one fell. People *left*. Suddenly. Quietly. And they didn't all come back."

There was a long pause. Then:

"I don't talk about it," Celia said. "It's not my place."

But she didn't stop talking, either.

***

Annabel sipped her tea. Outside, the sun had shifted, casting long shadows across the village green.

She stood to leave, nodding to Bernard — who gave the faintest of nods back, like a man who already knew more than he wanted to.

It was as she turned toward the door that she saw it.

Pinned to the Hare & Hound's corkboard, nestled between a flyer for ballroom dancing and a notice about lost spectacles, was a paper programme.

Old. Yellowed at the edges. Slightly curled.

"A Midsummer Night's Dream – Briarley Estate Players – Summer Gala, 2003."

Annabel stepped closer. The cast list was faded, the ink bleeding at the edges. She scanned the names.

And stopped.

Near the bottom.

Assistant Stage Manager: L. Ashcroft.

A name no one had mentioned this week.

But she had seen it — scribbled in Theo's notebook yesterday afternoon, just visible under his scarf during a rehearsal break.

And this morning, Leo Marks had pulled something from his pocket outside the post office — quickly, like he didn't want her to see it. She hadn't seen the full name, but the curve of the handwriting was... familiar.

She turned toward Bernard. "Who put that up?"

He didn't look up. "No idea. Wasn't there yesterday."

***

Outside, the breeze carried the scent of roses and rain.

Persephone was waiting on the windowsill of Honeystone Cottage, tail flicking, gaze fixed toward Briarley.

Not all performances began with a spotlight.

Some started in the corner of a pub, under a curl of paper, with a name that shouldn't be there.

Chapter 4

The second day of rehearsals began with Clarissa refusing to come out of the changing tent until someone located her "emotional support brooch," and a faerie child crying because someone else had eaten the last strawberry yoghurt.

By ten thirty, the sun was already melting makeup and patience in equal measure.

Annabel had brought her own chair today — folding canvas, sturdy — and placed it precisely two metres from the edge of the temporary stage. She called it her "neutral zone." Others called it ominous.

Persephone, stretched at her feet like a coiled ribbon of feline judgment, had already hissed twice and hadn't blinked once.

***

Theo stood centre stage; arms raised like Moses directing a scene change.

"People," he said, "the forest scene is sacred. It's where magic takes root. We cannot — *must not* — stumble through it like a tour group at a garden centre."

"Tell that to the stag beetle in my sleeve," muttered Jasper.

Olivia stepped forward, Helena script fluttering in one hand.

"I still think the faerie lights should pulse with the rhythm of the language," she said. "We're losing the poetry."

"We're losing the will to live," someone else said under their breath.

***

Annabel made notes quietly. And watched.

Leo Marks was standing near the sound booth, but he wasn't adjusting anything. He wasn't even pretending to take notes today. Instead, he kept glancing across the lawn — not at the actors, but toward the tree line.

Annabel followed his gaze. Nothing moved. Not yet.

She flipped her notebook to a clean page. The top line read simply:

L. Ashcroft.

***

Mid-rehearsal, a break was called when the wrong version of Act Two appeared in half the scripts.

Juliet stormed across the lawn holding the offending pages in one hand and a half-eaten croissant in the other.

"These aren't my copies," she barked at Theo.

"They came from your printer," he replied, without turning.

"I never added a monologue about Oberon's fear of birds."

Clarissa appeared behind a backdrop and loudly said, "I rather liked it."

Theo turned slowly. "We're doing *Shakespeare*, not free verse trauma therapy."

Annabel watched him closely.

His face had flushed slightly. His smile was brittle at the edges.

Someone had touched the script.

Someone had edited it — and not for the first time.

***

During the break, Annabel wandered behind the set tents. The ground was softer here, trodden with footprints. The trees cast long shadows, even in the morning sun.

A kettle was boiling on the tea table. No one stood near it.

Annabel reached into her satchel and pulled out the old programme. The name was still there. *L. Ashcroft.*

She turned it over.

Someone had written in pencil, faint but deliberate:

"Truth is never silent. It waits for the line."

***

"Annabel?"

She looked up.

Bettany stood a few feet away, a stack of costume alterations in her arms.

"Can I help you?"

Annabel smiled politely. "Just avoiding another speech about forest symbolism."

Bettany's eyes dropped to the paper in Annabel's hand.

For a moment, her face didn't move.

Then she turned and walked away without saying another word.

***

Annabel folded the programme and tucked it back into her bag.

Behind her, Persephone let out a low growl. Not a hiss — deeper. Like a warning.

Someone had changed the script.

Someone didn't want the past to stay buried.

And someone was watching the performance more carefully than they should.

Chapter 5

The air had changed.

The second day of rehearsals had started cooler — a breeze twisting through the trees around Briarley Estate, tugging at the edge of backdrops and scattering pages that hadn't been weighted properly.

Annabel had noticed the actors were quieter. Less posturing. Even Clarissa had refrained from quoting herself in the third person.

Something in the atmosphere had gone still.

***

She found Bernard just off the side lawn, behind the drinks table, methodically slicing lemons into quarters as if they'd personally offended him.

"Bit early for cocktails, isn't it?" she asked.

He didn't look up.

"They've asked for cucumber water," he muttered. "Cucumber. This isn't a spa. It's a village."

Annabel smiled, then lowered her voice.

"Did you see the programme I found in the pub?"

He hesitated — just a fraction of a second — then continued slicing.

"Wasn't mine to find," he said.

"But someone pinned it up."

Bernard finally looked up.

"I don't know who put it there. I didn't ask. And if you're smart, you won't either."

There was weight in that. Old weight.

Annabel studied him. "L. Ashcroft. She worked the old production, didn't she?"

He wiped his hands on a cloth. "She did. So did others. None of them stuck around."

"Why?"

He picked up a fresh lemon.

"Some stories just don't like being told twice."

***

The rehearsal resumed slowly. Voices flat. Blocking stilted. Even Theo was subdued — checking his phone more often than his cues.

Then a crate appeared near the props table. Not marked. Not listed. Not claimed.

Theo looked at it, frowned, and turned to Juliet. "Did you bring this up from storage?"

She shook her head. "Haven't been near the shed today."

"Well, someone—"

Clarissa let out a sudden gasp.

She'd opened the crate.

Inside was a faded green velvet waistcoat, the edges frayed, buttons mismatched. A costume piece. Old. And stitched just inside the collar, in pale thread:

H.M.

No one spoke.

Then Kitty — silent until now — stepped back so suddenly her heel caught on a stone. She stumbled. Caught herself.

Annabel moved toward her. "Are you—?"

"I'm fine," Kitty said quickly. Too quickly.

She turned and walked away without another word.

Theo looked back into the crate. "Who the hell is H.M.?"

No one answered.

***

That afternoon, in the Hare & Hound, Ronnie was telling Henry that someone had been seen at the station the night before. Just standing. Watching the platform.

"Didn't get on," he said. "Didn't get off, either. Just waited. Asked if the train to London was on time. Then disappeared."

"Visitor?" Henry asked.

"Stranger," Ronnie replied.

He didn't say more. But the word hung there like a note that hadn't resolved.

***

Back at Honeystone Cottage, the windows were closed against the chill and the kettle had begun to mutter. Persephone sat like a queen near the bookcase, tail swishing with faint disapproval.

Annabel spread out her notes on the kitchen table.

The programme.

The edits.

The quote: *Truth is never silent. It waits for the line.*

She opened Theo's script, flipping through the forest scene again.

There — a single line, subtly altered.

"For night's swift dragons cut the clouds full fast"

...was now written as:

"Night's dragons circle, but the truth burns faster."

No red pen. No note. But the curve of the handwriting... it was precise. Academic.

She'd seen it before.

***

As she sat back, the door creaked. Not open — just... creaked.

Then, soft as a breath, something slid through the letterbox and landed on the mat.

Annabel stood. Crossed the room. Picked it up.

No envelope. Just a folded slip of paper.

Inside, one line:

"Some truths won't wait for Act Five."

Chapter 6

The third day of rehearsals began late.

Theo arrived after everyone else, which in itself was enough to shift the mood. He wore the same scarf from the day before, wrapped tighter than the weather required, and his sunglasses stayed on even as clouds rolled across the sun.

Annabel clocked all of it — the way he flinched at applause during warm-ups, the way he missed a cue from Juliet and pretended not to — but said nothing. She simply took her chair near the trellis, notebook open, Persephone curled like punctuation at her feet.

⁕

It was Clarissa who cracked first.

They were running the scene where Titania first sees Bottom — the part where magic and madness start to mix — when she paused mid-line and stared at the tree line.

Her voice, usually three parts drama and one part thunder, softened.

"You know," she said, almost as if to herself, "this is exactly how she played it."

The cast stilled.

Annabel looked up. Theo didn't.

"Who?" someone asked.

Clarissa blinked. Realized she had spoken aloud. "No one. Forget it."

Juliet narrowed her eyes. "You mean... *Hannah*, don't you?"

Silence. Theo turned his head, just slightly. His jaw was tight.

Clarissa shook her head once, sharply. "No one's said that name in twenty years for good reason."

"But she was in the original production, right?" Jasper asked. "I remember my mum saying—"

"Drop it," Theo said.

And just like that, the rehearsal ended.

***

Annabel didn't follow the others when they scattered for tea and murmured excuses. She stayed where she was, notebook open, the name *Hannah* already written twice.

She'd felt it — like something shifted in the soil under the estate. Like a tremor of memory.

***

She found Theo later, sitting on the edge of the makeshift stage, staring out toward the trees.

"You should be inside," she said gently.

"I should be a lot of things," he muttered.

She stood beside him. Waited.

Finally, he said, "She was the kind of girl that made people think about songs. Even if they didn't sing."

"Hannah?"

He nodded.

"She was only supposed to be here for the summer. She had a voice like honey and a face that made even Clarissa nervous. Everyone loved her. Even if they didn't mean to."

"Did you?"

"I was sixteen," he said. "She smiled at me once and I forgot my own name."

He looked up at the branches above. "One night, she was meant to meet someone. She told me to wait under the lilacs."

Annabel's eyes widened. "Wait—"

"I waited," Theo said. "She never came."

***

Later that night, Annabel returned to Honeystone Cottage, opened her notebook, and wrote a single line beneath Hannah's name:

"She was meant to meet someone."

She circled it twice.

Then she looked at the other note —

the one that had arrived under her door

the night before.

"Some truths won't wait for Act Five."

She flipped the page.

And began writing a new cast list.

Not of characters.

But of secrets.

Chapter 7

The Hare & Hound was quieter than usual for a late afternoon, but the air buzzed with the same low voltage that always came before a storm — or a scandal.

Annabel took her tea by the window, notebook closed, listening.

Henry was behind the bar, restocking tonic water. Celia Ward and Mrs. Gilchrist were at their usual table, nursing teas that had long gone cold. Ronnie sat a few stools down from Bernard, who was pretending not to listen while polishing the same glass he'd started on that morning.

✳✳✳

It didn't take long.

Celia leaned forward, low voice already high with thrill.

"I told you, didn't I, Maureen? I *told* you she'd come up again. You can't just *erase* a girl like that."

Mrs. Gilchrist sniffed. "I didn't say they erased her. I said they never told the *truth*. There's a difference."

Ronnie made a sound halfway between a cough and a chuckle. "You lot were convinced she ran off to Hollywood. Or joined a cult."

"She *might* have," Celia snapped. "Strange things happened in that summer. And she wasn't from here. People like that don't stay. They stir the pot and leave someone else to clean up."

Annabel sipped her tea. "What was her name?"

All three froze.

Then Celia said, a little too casually, "*Hannah.* Pretty little thing. Bit too pretty, if you ask me."

****

"She wasn't *meant* for here," Mrs. Gilchrist added. "You don't drop a girl like that into a village and expect peace."

"What do you mean?" Annabel asked.

"She made men nervous. And women furious. Looked at people like she was reading their diary. Wore red lipstick before ten a.m. and didn't blush about it."

"She had this way," Ronnie said quietly, "of making you think she was listening. Even when she wasn't."

Annabel turned to him. "Did you talk to her?"

He shrugged.

"Delivered her letters, mostly. I remember the envelopes — pink paper, sometimes lavender-scented. One had glitter inside. She always smiled. But she looked... tired. Like she knew something was coming."

***

At that moment, the pub door opened, and a boy wandered in. Thin, muddy trainers, curly hair, probably ten at most.

"Gareth!" Henry called. "Your gran's looking for you."

Gareth ignored him. He spotted Annabel and made a beeline to her table.

"You're the professor, aren't you?"

Annabel nodded slowly. "I am."

"My mum says you're asking questions about the play. About the one from ages ago."

"I am. Why?"

Gareth grinned, missing one tooth. "My dad told me a story once. Said when *he* was a kid, he saw a girl dancing on the lawn at night. All in white. Said she looked like a ghost."

Annabel blinked. "Where?"

"Near the orchard. Briarley." He looked immensely pleased. "Said she smiled right at him and then disappeared behind the trees."

Celia rolled her eyes. "Don't fill her head with fairy tales, Gareth."

"It wasn't a fairy tale," he said. "Dad said she was real. Said no one believed him. Said her name was Hannah."

***

When Gareth left, Henry refilled Annabel's cup without asking.

"She made an impression," he said.

"Seems like it."

"Some people remember her too clearly," he added. "Others not at all. That's how you know there's a lie underneath."

Annabel looked up.

He gave her a small, unreadable smile.

"Memories don't fade like that on their own."

Chapter 8

Rehearsal ended early.

The lines had fallen flat. The rhythm was off.

Clarissa claimed she could feel a storm in her joints. No one argued.

Theo didn't speak as the cast dispersed.

He stood at the edge of the lawn, arms crossed tightly over his chest, staring into the trees as if expecting someone to step out and explain the day to him.

Annabel watched him from a distance. She made a note: *"There's something in his silence now — not just*

pressure. Memory."

***

By dusk, the estate had emptied, save for the lingering buzz of insects and the slow whisper of summer grass.

Theo walked.

Not with purpose. More like sleepwalking.

He didn't notice how far he'd gone until the orchard opened around him — wide and silvered in moonlight. The same orchard Gareth's father had once spoken of.

There was music.

Soft. Distant. Old.

He turned, frowning.

It wasn't from the house. It was closer. Like a radio hidden under the leaves. Or a memory with its own speaker.

The song wasn't familiar — not exactly. But something about it—

He stopped.

***

She used to dance here.

He could see her.

Not truly — but in the shape of the wind, the light pooling on the grass.

Barefoot. Spinning slowly. White dress catching the moon. Hair a little wild, mouth curved into a smile like she'd stolen it from the stars.

Hannah.

Theo's breath hitched. He hadn't said her name aloud in years.

"She danced like she had no idea anyone was watching.

But I was.

And someone else was too."

****

He sat on a half-buried bench, hands trembling.

The music looped and faded.

Something shifted in his mind — a locked door rattling.

He remembered the lilacs.

He remembered waiting.

He remembered the way her eyes had looked that night — not bright, but anxious. How she'd squeezed his hand, just once, before telling him *"I need to speak to someone first."*

And then—

A voice.

Low. Male. Sharp.

He hadn't seen the face, only the shape. A man stepping between the trees. Hannah turning, voice tight.

"Not now. I said *no.*"

Theo had looked away then. A sixteen-year-old boy who knew love from poetry, not real life.

And when he looked back?

She was gone.

***

He stood now; his breath caught in his throat.

His hand brushed something on the bench beside him — soft, brittle.

A single, dried violet.

He stared at it.

Then heard it — a branch snapping in the dark.

He turned.

Nothing.

No one.

Just the whisper of leaves.

But he felt it.

Someone was there.

Watching.

Just like before.

***

You left and no one screamed.

Not even me.

That's the thing I think about most.
Not the orchard. Not the rumours. Not
the newspaper article that wasn't even an
article. Just a paragraph tucked beside a

column about dog show winners and rising milk prices.

You were worth more than that.

You were worth more than the silence they wrapped you in.

They all remember you differently now. You're like a dream they half-pretend to have had. Some say you were trouble. Some say you were sweet. One of them still tells people you were meant to be famous. They use your name like it's a spice. Just a pinch. Nothing too strong.

But I remember the girl who danced barefoot on wet grass, even when your ankles hurt.

Who smelled like violets because you pressed them in every book. Even the scripts.

Who said you never wanted to be the centre of the stage — just *heard.*

I've kept your lines, Hannah.

The real ones.

The ones they cut. The ones they mocked. The ones you whispered to me in the dark, thinking maybe the story would let you live longer if you rewrote it yourself.

I know now why you asked him to wait under the lilacs.

And I know who got there first.

So, I brought them back.

The players. The liars. The ones who clapped too late and mourned too quietly.

I gave them the same stage. Same lines. Same masks.

And now I'm waiting to see who forgets their script first.

They've all had twenty years.

But this time, the last act will be the truth.

I promise you that.

Chapter 9

Theo didn't sleep.

He sat on the edge of his bed until dawn painted shadows across the floor. The violet lay on the desk, dried and silent. He hadn't touched it again.

He didn't need to.

The images had come back in waves — flashes, sounds, fragments of emotion that didn't feel like his own.

A shadow in the orchard.

A voice that wasn't hers.

The way Hannah's fingers trembled when she'd handed him the note.

The way she looked over her shoulder, as if someone was always a step behind her.

***

By the time he arrived at Briarley for rehearsal, he looked... thinner. Like part of him hadn't come back from the night before.

Annabel noticed immediately.

She was already there, sipping coffee and taking notes, Persephone sunbathing in a chair like royalty. She watched Theo the way a cat watches a mouse trying to convince itself it's not being watched.

He avoided her eyes.

***

Juliet ran a warm-up, Clarissa demanded new blocking, and the forest scene fell apart twice before lunch.

Theo snapped during Scene Three.

"No, no, no — it's not about flowers and wings, it's about *illusion!* Love as a trick. Desire as a spell. You don't trust the magic. You surrender to it."

Olivia blinked. "Theo—?"

He stepped back. Closed his eyes.

"Take ten," he muttered. And walked off the lawn.

Annabel found him near the prop tent, pacing like he was trying to outrun a thought.

"You remember something," she said.

He didn't look at her.

"It's blurry," he admitted. "But I saw her that night. Not just in the orchard. Earlier. She was nervous. Not scared exactly. More like... tense. Like she was holding something in."

Annabel waited.

"She gave me a note. Told me to wait. Said she had to meet someone first. I thought it was about a boyfriend or something. I was sixteen, I thought everything was about romance."

He paused.

"But I heard something. After she left me. In the trees. A man's voice. Low. Angry. I didn't think about it then. Didn't *want* to think about it."

He turned toward her, eyes tired.

"I think I saw the last person who spoke to her."

***

They both fell silent as Victor Lang, the lighting technician, appeared from behind the tent.

Corduroy trousers. Always slightly out of sync with the rest of the group.

He nodded politely, but Theo stiffened.

Annabel clocked it.

Victor paused. "Something wrong?"

Theo shook his head too quickly. "No. Just tired."

Victor looked at Annabel. "I remember you from the first day," he said. "You asked about the 2003 show. I didn't think anyone still cared."

Annabel offered a smile. "History has a habit of repeating itself."

Victor smiled back, but it didn't reach his eyes.

He walked away.

Theo exhaled.

"It might've been his voice I heard. Or someone who sounded like him."

***

That night, Annabel sat in her kitchen at Honeystone Cottage, re-reading her notebook. She drew a line from Hannah's name to Theo's. Then another, toward Victor's.

Persephone meowed once. Looked toward the window.

Annabel got up.

Outside, on the sill, was another violet.

Fresh.

This time, there was no note.

She opened the window.

And stared into the dark, listening.

But the night was as quiet as a stage

before the curtain rises.

Chapter 10

Theo didn't arrive for rehearsal.

At first, it didn't seem unusual. He was often late, often moody, and always scattered. But by ten-thirty, the cast had started buzzing. Clarissa was pacing. Olivia kept checking her phone. Jasper had already suggested staging a rebellion and forming a co-op theatre collective without him.

Annabel said nothing.

She simply looked toward the orchard.

***

She texted him twice. No reply.

She called. Straight to voicemail.

By eleven, the whispers had spread from the green to the prop tent to the steps of the Hare & Hound. By noon, even Bernard had heard.

"He's never missed a rehearsal before," Clarissa muttered. "Not even the day Juliet threatened to throw a smoke bomb at Olivia."

Henry, pouring cider for a pair of WI members, leaned across the bar toward Annabel.

"He didn't come in for breakfast. Usually has toast. Quiet, like he's trying to dissolve into it."

Annabel nodded. "He's not answering his phone."

"Should we worry?" Celia asked loudly from a corner table. "Or is this part of the whole *'art as suffering'* thing?"

Annabel stood. "I think it's time someone checked the estate."

***

The housekeeper at Briarley was polite, if slightly confused.

Theo's room was untouched since the night before.

Bed unmade. Mug half-full on the nightstand. His satchel still on the chair.

His phone wasn't there. Neither was Theo.

A light breeze had blown the window curtains open. On the writing desk sat one thing, and one thing only.

A single sheet of paper.

Annabel stepped closer. It wasn't a note. Not a script page. Not even theatre-related.

Just one sentence, in careful script.

"She said she'd meet me under the lilacs."

Annabel exhaled slowly. The words weren't meant for her. But they were left for someone.

***

By evening, the cast had grown restless.

Juliet claimed Theo was "pulling a method acting vanishing act."

Olivia wasn't speaking.

Victor was... watching.

Annabel stood just outside the rehearsal tent, listening to Clarissa attempt a speech about "professionalism in the face of mild chaos."

She didn't go home that night.

Instead, she walked back to the orchard. Alone.

The trees rustled faintly.

The moon rose, like an eye.

And far off, near the lilac grove, she saw something white fluttering in the dark.

A scrap of fabric.

Or a memory.

She didn't go closer.

Not yet.

Chapter 11

By morning, the whispers about Theo had grown teeth.

Clarissa was already workshopping a press statement ("He has... artistic tendencies. Emotional fragility. We stand with him.").

Juliet had suggested postponing rehearsals until "we find the body — I mean, find him."

Annabel didn't speak.

She packed her satchel. She filled Persephone's bowl. And she walked straight into the village square like a woman with a shopping list and murder in her eyes.

***

She found Victor Lang at the side of the set, tinkering with a lighting rig that didn't need fixing.

"Victor," she said, voice level. "How long have you known Theo?"

He hesitated. "Since... 2003. We met during the original production."

"You were there when Hannah was."

His mouth twitched.

"You remember her?"

"Everyone remembers her."

"That's not what I asked."

He put down his tools. "She was...
intense. In a way people mistook for
confidence. But she was scared. I saw it."

"Did you ever speak to her that
night?"

"No."

Too quick.

Annabel tilted her head. "Did you
hear anything?"

"I went home early."

Another lie.

"I think Theo remembered your
voice."

Victor's eyes snapped to hers.

She said nothing more.

He turned and walked away.

***

Annabel bought a raspberry tart she didn't want and leaned on the counter of the bakery of Bea Simmons.

"Did you know Hannah?" she asked to Mrs Gilchrist who was serving the clients.

Mrs. Gilchrist, not even blinking, said, "She ordered lemon curd tarts and always said thank you. That's more manners than some."

"People said she was trouble."

"She made people feel things. That's what they meant."

Annabel nodded. "Did you see her after that last rehearsal?"

"No. But my husband said he heard shouting. Near the orchard."

"Who?"

"He never told me."

She paused. "But he stopped going up there after that. Said it felt... wrong."

***

Ronnie, the Postman, handed her a stack of letters meant for next door. "You're chasing shadows, Professor."

"Shadows don't leave violets on my windowsill."

He paused. "Hannah used to send letters to herself."

Annabel blinked. "What?"

"She told me it helped. Writing down what she wanted someone to say to her, and mailing it. Said it made her feel... less forgotten."

He scratched his head. "I don't think they ever arrived, though."

***

Annabel stopped by the hall of the Women's Institute on her way back toward Briarley. The door was open, and the warm scent of old fabric, weak tea, and lavender polish curled out like a memory.

Inside, a woman stood at a long table, folding stage costumes into neatly labelled boxes. She wore a cardigan the colour of oatmeal and had a scarf wrapped loosely around her neck, even though it wasn't cold. Her hair was pinned up, her movements careful.

"Hello?" Annabel said gently.

The woman looked up. Her face was familiar, though Annabel couldn't place why. Early forties, maybe. Quiet eyes. Watchful, but kind.

"You're the professor," the woman said, not quite a question.

"I am. You're helping with the play?"

The woman nodded once. "Just the costumes. Sorting the old ones. Some are from the last time."

Annabel tilted her head. "You were involved with the original production?"

"A little." Her smile flickered. "I did odd jobs. Mostly quiet work. I was young."

She folded a piece of silk with particular care. It was violet — deep and soft, with faint embroidery at the collar.

"Did you know Hannah?" Annabel asked.

The woman's hands paused. Just a second. Barely noticeable.

"She was very... memorable."

Annabel waited, but no more came.

After a moment, the woman looked up. "Some stories are better left in the dressing room," she said. "No offense."

"None taken."

The woman smiled again, smaller this time. "Sorry. Tea's gone cold. I should finish this."

She left through the back, quiet as a thought.

***

She walked out alone to the storage shed behind Briarley late afternoon.

It was cluttered with set pieces, props, half-built archways, and old script boxes.

She opened one marked 2003.

Dust. Curling pages. Ink-stained envelopes.

And there, folded inside a costume bodice: a letter.

Sealed. Violet wax.

Initials: H.R.

Not Theo's.

Not Victor's.

Not anyone she'd heard mentioned.

She opened it.

"Meet me under the lilacs. Please. I can't leave until I know the truth."

—H

***

Annabel exhaled slowly.

She looked out across the estate. The trees were silent.

But the secrets?

They were finally starting to speak.

Chapter 12

She sat at the kitchen table, teacup cooling beside her notebook.

Persephone perched on the windowsill, tail twitching, eyes fixed on something Annabel couldn't see.

"You are tense," Annabel said.

Persephone flicked an ear, unimpressed.

Evie appeared in the doorway holding a slice of toast and an expression halfway between concern and challenge.

"You've got that look," she said.

"What look?"

"The 'I'm about to kick over someone's perfectly arranged lie' look."

Annabel half-smiled. "It's a good morning for truth."

Evie sat down. "You're thinking about Hannah again."

"She left everything behind."

"Or someone left it behind for her."

That gave Annabel pause. Then: "Either way, it's still here. I'm going to look."

Persephone meowed, short and sharp.

Evie nodded at the cat. "That's approval. Or a threat. It's hard to tell."

***

The prop shed smelled like dust, paint, and silence.

Annabel stood just inside the doorway, eyes adjusting to the dim light that sliced through warped wooden slats. Behind her, the summer breeze fluttered the edge of a cracked canvas backdrop — a painted forest, faded now. Dreamlike. Unreal.

Much like the stories she'd been hearing all day.

Persephone, of course, had followed.

She paced the threshold of the shed like a sentry — tail high, eyes narrowed, refusing to step inside.

Annabel glanced at her. "Bad memories?"

The cat sat, curled her tail around her paws, and stared directly at the suitcase.

Annabel opened it anyway.

***

She had asked five people where Hannah went after the play ended in 2003.

No one could agree.

"Back to Ireland, I think."

"Paris. She had a cousin there."

"Brighton. Maybe?"

"Someone said she had a man waiting for her in Spain."

Not one of them could name the cousin.

Not one could remember what Hannah wore the last day she was seen.

But all of them said it with certainty.

As if that certainty had been handed to them.

Wrapped in ribbon.

Labelled: *"We don't talk about this."*

***

Annabel ran her hand along a shelf until her fingers brushed canvas.

A suitcase.

Old, pale green, with one corner fraying. She crouched, undid the latch.

Inside, everything was folded.

Delicate. Precise.

A white cotton blouse. Stage shoes with scuffed toes. A violet scarf. A mirror wrapped in a tea towel. A tiny bottle of perfume — half full.

Annabel lifted it. Uncapped it.

The scent of violets bloomed in the air.

***

She sat back on her heels, heart steady, fury cold and quiet.

If Hannah had run away, she would've taken this with her.

She would've packed in a hurry. Or not at all.

But this wasn't abandonment.

This was a pause that never stopped.

***

There was a script tucked inside the mirror's towel.

A sticky note still clung to the back.

"Don't forget your lines. Or they'll rewrite you."

Her handwriting.

Sharp and swooping and alive.

Annabel exhaled.

"She didn't leave."

"She was erased."

***

Back at the pub, Celia was regaling a few locals with another version of *The Tale of Hannah, The Runaway* that evening.

Annabel set the scarf down in the centre of their table.

"She left this," she said, voice calm. "And everything else. Folded. Clean. Packed."

Celia blinked. "So?"

"If she was going to Paris, or Brighton, or even the moon, don't you think she'd have taken her shoes?"

No one replied.

Annabel leaned in slightly.

"You all say she left. Then tell me: where did she go?"

No one could answer.

The silence was the loudest thing in the room.

***

Later that evening at Honeystone Cottage, Evie poured her a glass of wine. "You found it."

"Neatly folded. Like someone expected her to come back."

"And when she didn't?"

Annabel looked at Persephone, who was pawing delicately at the scarf on the table.

"They folded her story up, too."

Chapter 13

It had started with music.

A few soft notes, floating on the breeze like perfume.

Theo had followed the sound, thinking someone had left a speaker on — some director's idea of mood-building. But the music was wrong. Not from the current show. It was *theirs. In 2003.*

A track Hannah used to hum when she was nervous.

Theo's skin had gone cold even as the night air stayed warm. He'd stepped beyond the edge of the rehearsal green, down the sloping path toward the orchard.

And then the world shifted.

A footfall behind him.

The scent of violets.

A voice — low, unfamiliar. Or was it?

"You should've forgotten."

Something hit the back of his head.

And everything turned to silence.

***

Now he woke in the dark.

Not pitch dark — there was light, somewhere. A crack beneath a door? A sliver through the boards?

He sat up slowly. The back of his head throbbed.

Concrete floor. Wooden beams. Damp air. An old wine cellar? A basement?

His heart kicked.

He wasn't tied. Not yet.

His phone was gone.

No windows. No sound.

He stood, swaying slightly, and checked the door. Locked.

He pressed his ear to it. Nothing.

Except... footsteps, somewhere above. Slow. Deliberate.

***

His pulse roared.

Hannah.

Her voice. That night.

"Meet me under the lilacs."

He had waited. He had watched her walk away.

He had heard a voice. Not hers. Not gentle.

Angry. Male. Familiar.

Victor? No.

Jasper? Maybe.

Someone older?

He never turned around that night.

He'd convinced himself it didn't matter.

But now...

Now he was locked underground and someone had made it matter again.

***

Theo crouched in the corner. Pulled his knees to his chest.

Not just fear.

Guilt.

He had forgotten. Not on purpose. Not cruelly.

Just... safely.

And now, the truth had caught up.

Maybe Hannah never left.

Maybe someone had made sure *she couldn't.*

And maybe that same someone had just made the same promise to him.

"You should've forgotten."

***

Twenty years.

That's how long it stayed quiet.

Long enough for people to forget the shape of her voice. Long enough for the lies to settle like dust on an unused stage.

And now they want to do it all again.

The same play. The same lines.

But this time... they keep saying her name like it's sacred. Like she was the victim.

Hannah.

Hannah, who laughed too loud.

Hannah, who looked at everyone like she saw right through them.

Hannah, who was supposed to leave.

But she didn't.

She made things *complicated.*

And now Theo, of all people — little Theo, who barely understood what he saw — starts remembering.

He waited under the lilacs. That's all he was supposed to do. Just wait.

But then he talked.

And now Annabel — with her notebooks and her cat and her damned questions — is picking at threads that were never meant to be pulled.

They shouldn't be doing this play.

They shouldn't be talking about her.

Because the last time they did...

someone died.

Chapter 14

Annabel stared at the envelope again.

The wax seal had cracked when she opened it, the violet wax now a faint stain on the paper.

The initials were still clear: H.R.

No last name. No address. Just a short, urgent message and a signature that felt like a ghost breathing through time.

She'd checked the cast list from 2003 twice. No H.R.

Not among the leads. Not backstage. Not crew.

So, who wrote it?

Or rather... who did Hannah write it
for?

***

Evie hovered in the kitchen, biting the corner of a biscuit. "Could it be her real name? Maybe Hannah was short for something?"

Annabel shook her head. "Everyone knew her as Hannah. Even Theo. She wouldn't have signed a private note with initials no one used."

Evie raised a brow. "Then it's someone else. Someone important enough that Hannah didn't write their full name. Someone *she didn't want found out."*

On the windowsill, Persephone sneezed loudly, as if to say *finally, you're catching up.*

***

The village registry was kept in a cabinet behind the clerk's desk at the parish office. It smelled of parchment, mildew, and misfiled secrets.

Annabel flipped through the 2003 entries.

A few names jumped out — births, deaths, a wedding or two.

And then, tucked at the bottom of a page from midsummer:

"Harriet Rowe – Temporary guest of Briarley Estate, volunteer, stage assistant."

Annabel circled the name.

H.R.

Not cast. Not crew. Not remembered.

Forgotten... deliberately?

***

Mrs. Gilchrist was in her usual bakery spot when Annabel returned.

"Harriet Rowe," Annabel said.

The older woman looked up from her crossword. "That name's a wrinkle. Haven't heard it in years."

"She was helping with the play in 2003. Listed as a volunteer."

Mrs. Gilchrist made a face. "Quiet girl. Never said much. Wore brown like it was a uniform. But she followed Hannah around like a moon orbiting the sun. In love with her, probably."

Annabel blinked. "Do you know what happened to her?"

Mrs. Gilchrist shrugged. "Left the day after Hannah disappeared. No goodbye. Just gone."

***

That night, Annabel sat with her notebook open, the name Harriet Rowe circled again and again.

H.R. was here.

H.R. followed Hannah.

H.R. vanished the next day.

Persephone jumped onto the table and pawed at a loose sheet of paper.

Underneath it was a photograph — one Annabel had taken from the programme archive.

The cast of 2003, blurry, sunlit, happy.

But in the background, just behind Hannah's shoulder... a young woman in brown.

Watching.

Expression unreadable.

Chapter 15

Clarissa Fairmont held the scarf between two fingers like it was made of mould and regret.

"She always wore violet," she said. "Even when it clashed."

She didn't mention the time she told Hannah that stage makeup wasn't enough to "cover up that face built to ruin men." She didn't mention how Hannah had laughed. Or how Clarissa had thrown the blush brush against the mirror after she left.

Now, she looked at the scarf like it had grown teeth.

"She wasn't right for Titania, you know. Too soft. Too... sincere."

She dropped it on the table and walked away.

***

Jasper stirred sugar into his coffee like he needed it to drown.

"She had a way of making you feel like the centre of something," he said. "Even if you weren't."

He remembered the garden party. Hannah in white, swaying to music no one else heard. Harriet Rowe sitting on the bench nearby, watching like her life depended on it.

He'd smiled at Hannah.

He'd never noticed Harriet leave.

Until the next day, when neither of them came back.

***

Kitty Simmons still had the necklace.

Hannah had left it in the dressing room one night — a tiny silver thing with a glass bead in the centre. Kitty had meant to return it.

Then the next day, she'd been gone.

Kitty never wore it. But she never threw it away.

Now she held it in her palm and wondered, for the thousandth time, if *that night* was when she made her worst mistake.

Not seeing.

Not stopping.

Or seeing... and walking the other way.

***

Juliet Hayes hadn't known Hannah.

But she knew what it felt like to have eyes on you all the time. Eyes that judged. Eyes that lingered.

She watched Annabel move around the stage now like a detective in ballet flats. Watched the older cast go pale whenever a new question was asked.

She thought about how easy it would be to love someone like Hannah.

And how much easier it might have been to hate her.

***

The killer sat by the river just past dusk, holding the photograph between shaking fingers.

Harriet. Hannah. Both smiling.

Neither looking at the camera.

They held it over the lighter for a second too long.

"I thought it was over," they whispered.

"I thought we buried this with her."

The flame curled the edges of memory.

But the guilt?

That didn't burn.

Chapter 16

Annabel didn't return to the estate right away.

Instead, she took the long path around the village, notebook tucked under her arm, Persephone following at a lazy pace like a tiny shadow with opinions.

She wasn't sure what she was looking for.

But she knew the feeling — the whisper of a thought that wouldn't sit still.

***

The archives at the church hall were dusty and over-organized. The vicar had insisted everything be preserved after the last fire alarm false-alarmed the fire brigade into nearly bulldozing the old photo wall.

Annabel ran her fingers along the rows of labelled boxes until she found it:

"2003 – Summer Events – Briarley."

She sat cross-legged on the floor, Persephone curling nearby, and began flipping through the photos.

Garden parties. Rehearsals. Pub nights. Cast dinners. Stage chaos.

And then—

A wide group shot of the cast on the lawn.

Hannah, centre. Laughing. Arms draped over two younger actors, wild hair, the violet scarf around her neck.

And just behind her, almost hidden by the trees—

A girl.

Slight.

Watching.

Brown sweater. Eyes fixed on Hannah.

Not smiling.

Not part of the group.

Just... there.

***

Annabel's breath caught.

She leaned in closer. The face was younger. Softer. But familiar.

The woman from the WI.

The one folding costumes.

The one who said: *"Some stories are better left in the dressing room."*

She had been there.

Not just in the village. At the heart of it.

***

She flipped the photo over.

Three names were written in faded ink.

"Hannah M., Jasper W., Clarissa F."

Then scratched faintly underneath in
a different pen:

"H.R."

***

Annabel stared at the initials.

Her pulse slowed.

Everything sharpened.

She didn't forget Hannah.

She never left her.

Chapter 17

Annabel had barely tucked the photo back into her notebook when the knock came.

Evie stood at the door, out of breath, cheeks pink.

"Don't change clothes," she said. "Come now."

***

The train station had been shut down for a decade, but the platform still slouched in its patch of overgrown weeds, as if waiting for something it knew would never come.

Annabel and Evie reached it in twenty minutes flat.

"Theo was here," Evie said. "Ronnie said Mrs. Gilchrist saw someone. Tall, thin, pacing. Looked 'unsettled.' That was the word she used."

Annabel scanned the space. No Theo. No movement.

Just silence. And the rustle of dry leaves where a bench had collapsed into itself.

***

She walked the platform slowly.

Then she saw it.

On the edge of the bench, half-hidden in the weeds:

a torn piece of paper.

She crouched.

Not a receipt. Not litter.

A torn script page.

Old. Faded.

Typed lines and handwritten blocking.

Smudged in places.

Her breath caught as she recognized the play.

The one from 2003.

And in the margins, scrawled in Hannah's handwriting — the curved "H" unmistakable now — one single sentence:

"He said he'd protect me."

"But he lied."

***

"Annabel?"

Evie was watching her, brows furrowed.

"No sign of him," Annabel said, voice quiet.

She stood, paper in hand. Her eyes didn't leave the platform.

"If he was here," she added, "I don't think he was alone."

***

Back in the village, the WI hall was locked.

The costumes were gone.

The scarf was gone.

The violet scent? Faint.

Almost gone.

But not quite.

Harriet Rowe wasn't there.

And the bench at the station?

Might've held Theo.

Might've held someone else.

But whoever they were...

They had Hannah's script.

Chapter 18

Annabel didn't say a word when she returned from the train station.

She simply put the torn script page on the table beside her tea, watched Persephone sniff it with disdain, and said quietly,

"They're getting sloppy."

***

The next morning, she walked through the rehearsal tent with her notebook in hand, hair pinned up with surgical precision.

She smiled at Juliet. Thanked Victor for fixing the spotlight. Nodded at Clarissa like everything was fine.

And then she said, loud enough to be heard:

"I think it's time we performed the final scene. The one from 2003."

Silence.

"Just for us," she added. "A private run. As a tribute to Theo. And Hannah."

Clarissa's jaw twitched. Jasper looked at the ground.

Even Olivia — who didn't know half the story — suddenly looked like she'd swallowed her own tongue.

***

She assigned roles carefully.

Theo's part to Jasper.

Hannah's part to Juliet.

Every other cast member back into the costumes they'd worn twenty years ago — or the closest Annabel could find.

Evie watched it unfold with wide eyes.

"You're not really staging a memorial," she said later, while making sandwiches in Honeystone Cottage.

"I'm staging a pressure cooker," Annabel replied.

***

That afternoon, she returned to the WI.

The back door was open. The costume boxes were gone. The room smelled faintly of dust and violets.

A scarf — not Hannah's, but similar — lay draped across the back of a chair.

She touched it, then opened her notebook and wrote:

"She's still watching."

***

She pinned the final rehearsal announcement to the board in the pub that evening.

Final Scene Read-Through

Cast Only. Briarley. Saturday Night.

Beneath it, she wrote:

"No masks this time."

Chapter 19

Briarley had never felt so quiet.

The reading room smelled faintly of dust, lavender polish, and nerves.

Chairs were set in a circle.

Scripts were placed on each seat — copies of the final scene from the 2003 production.

The one no one remembered finishing.

The one Hannah never got to perform.

Juliet shuffled in first, eyes darting. Clarissa followed, already muttering about lighting. Jasper laughed too loudly at nothing.

Kitty looked pale.

Victor didn't speak.

Harriet... wasn't there. But Annabel wasn't surprised.

Yet.

***

She stood at the front, hands folded.

"This is a tribute," she said.

"To Theo, who is missing. To Hannah, who is remembered. To memory, which sometimes needs help."

"No audience. No direction. Just truth."

The cast opened their scripts.

Silence.

Then Juliet began.

***

"My love has vanished in the orchard's breath—"

"—And yet his shadow stands before me still."

Clarissa's voice cracked on her second line.

Jasper skipped three words, then went back.

Victor didn't speak at all.

***

Halfway through, Kitty stood.

"I'm sorry," she whispered. "I can't do this."

Annabel didn't stop her.

Because across the room, someone had just started crying.

Not loud.

Not theatrical.

Just a quiet, trembling sound that made everyone look.

It was Harriet.

No longer hidden.

No longer silent.

She had slipped into the room halfway through.

No one noticed.

Until now.

***

Juliet froze. "Who…?"

Clarissa's eyes narrowed. "She helped with costumes."

Harriet looked up. Her voice was barely audible.

"That scene… that wasn't fiction. That's what happened."

You could feel the air vanish.

Annabel stepped forward, calm as snowfall.

"Harriet," she said gently. "Do you want to tell us what happened after Hannah gave you her final lines?"

Harriet blinked.

"I didn't kill her."

"But I know who did."

Chapter 20

"I didn't kill her," Harriet said again, louder this time.

Her voice trembled, but she stayed on her feet.

In the centre of the rehearsal room.

Lit by nothing but a single overhead bulb and two decades of buried memory.

"But I saw what happened.

I saw where she went.

And who followed her."

***

Annabel didn't move.

She watched. She listened.

She noted everything — the way Clarissa's hands gripped the arms of her chair, the way Victor was no longer looking at Harriet but at the floor.

"We had just finished rehearsal," Harriet whispered.

"She said she needed to speak to someone. She didn't say who. Just that it was... important."

"She gave me a scarf to hold.

And a script to carry.

Said she'd be back in ten minutes."

"She never came back."

***

Juliet broke the silence. "Why didn't you tell anyone?"

Harriet swallowed. "Because someone told me not to."

Everyone stiffened.

"He came into the dressing room. He said Hannah had left. That she changed her mind. That she was never coming back."

"He said... if I talked about it, they'd think I was the reason."

"And I believed him."

∗∗∗

The room went still.

Clarissa's face was blank.

Jasper's jaw clenched.

Victor shifted.

And then — just as Annabel opened her mouth to speak — the lights snapped out.

Total darkness.

A gasp.

A crash.

A scream.

Then— Harriet's voice.

"He's here—!"

Another crash.

Chairs scraped the floor.

Something metal fell — a lighting stand, maybe.

Annabel shouted, "Evie, the lights!"

But Evie wasn't at the switchboard.

She was holding Harriet — blood on her sleeve.

Not much. But enough.

A scratch. A warning.

***

By the time the lights flickered back on, the attacker was gone.

Harriet stood shaking, tears and blood mixing on her scarf.

Someone had tried to shut her up.

And they'd failed.

But just barely.

***

Outside, in the shadows behind the garden hedge, a figure stood breathing heavily.

Watching.

Listening.

Knowing they'd waited too long.

"You should've kept quiet, Harriet."

"You should've let her stay buried."

They disappeared into the trees.

***

Far across the lawn, in the darkened library of Briarley, someone else watched the chaos from the window.

They folded a letter in perfect halves.

Violet-scented paper. A single pressed flower inside.

The backer.

"It's time," they whispered.

"No more curtain calls."

Chapter 22

Harriet's legs gave out like the truth had finally been too much to carry.

She collapsed into Evie's arms, her eyes fluttering, her lips moving but saying nothing.

"I've got her," Evie said, guiding her to the floor, careful, gentle.

Annabel dropped to her knees beside them, pressing two fingers to Harriet's wrist.

Pulse — faint but steady.

"She's not bleeding badly," she said. "It's the shock."

Persephone appeared out of nowhere, prowling across the floor as if summoned by drama, circling Harriet like a velvet omen.

The cast stood frozen.

Some in guilt.

Some in fear.

None of them moved to help.

***

"I'll call the doctor," Evie said, reaching for her phone.

Annabel nodded. "I need water. A cloth. Something—"

"I have something."

The voice came from behind.

***

She turned.

A man stood in the doorway. Mid-forties. Impeccably dressed. Bookish eyes behind thin glasses. A folded envelope in his hand.

"I believe," he said, "we need to speak."

Annabel stared. "You were at the pub. The day I asked about the 2003 performance."

He smiled softly. "I've been... nearby. My name is Simon Deane."

Persephone hissed.

"You're the backer."

He didn't deny it.

***

They stepped aside, just far enough for Annabel to hiss, "Why now? Why tonight?"

"Because the wrong person spoke first," he said, voice tight. "I was waiting. Planning. I wanted the truth in full, not fragments."

He handed her the envelope.

Inside was a photo. Hannah. Laughing.

And another woman beside her.

Harriet.

Younger.

Eyes fixed on Hannah like she was looking at the sun.

"I loved her," the backer whispered. "Not the way Harriet did. Not the way the men did. But I loved who she was. Her voice. Her honesty. I told her not to go to the orchard that night."

"She didn't listen."

***

Annabel opened her mouth — but behind them, someone shouted.

"Annabel!"

Evie. Panicked.

They turned.

Harriet was gone.

The scarf lay where she'd been.

The front door swung open — still moving, like a ghost had pushed it.

Chapter 23

Harriet ran.

Branches tore at her sleeves. Brambles clutched at her skirt. The forest floor rose up to meet her like it had been waiting twenty years for her return.

She didn't scream.

She didn't breathe.

She just ran.

***

Somewhere behind her — quiet. Precise. Certain — footsteps followed.

Not fast.

But never far.

"You couldn't let it rest," the voice echoed behind her.

"You had to bring her back."

***

The hem of her dress caught on a thornbush. Ripped.

She stumbled. Fell. Caught herself on her hands.

Dirt filled her nails. Blood smeared her palm.

She kept running.

The path twisted left — toward the orchard.

Of course it did.

***

Simon Deane stood with Annabel and Evie on the steps of Briarley, a strange, still horror sliding down his face like it had been thawing for years.

"She's reenacting it," he said quietly. "The same night. The same path."

Annabel's breath caught.

"And someone's following her."

***

They ran.

Evie grabbed the torch.

Simon took the map from the drawer — old, faded, annotated in his own handwriting.

"This way. The shortcut. If we're lucky—"

Annabel didn't wait for luck.

She sprinted.

***

Harriet's chest burned. Her eyes stung. Her legs screamed.

She reached the clearing — the place she last saw Hannah alive.

The moonlight spilled like memory across the grass.

"She was here," she whispered.

"She trusted me."

A sound behind her. A footstep. Too close.

She turned.

***

"You should've let her go," the voice said.

"You don't get to change the ending."

A glint of metal.

A breath.

Then—

"Harriet!"

Annabel's voice, slicing through the night.

A flashlight beam arced across the orchard.

The killer turned.

The blade dropped.

And Harriet — eyes wide — crumpled.

Not from the wound.

From the memory.

***

Simon reached her first.

Evie hit the killer with the torch. Not the beam. The handle.

Annabel caught Harriet before she hit the ground.

"It was them," Harriet whispered. "All this time. They told me I imagined it."

"You didn't," Annabel said.

"Not anymore."

Chapter 24

The study at Briarley was silent.

Outside, the trees whispered.

Inside, truth pressed at the windows like a storm begging to be let in.

Harriet sat near the fire, wrapped in Evie's shawl. Simon stood by the door; jaw clenched tight. Annabel sat across from the one person in the room who hadn't spoken since the chase ended.

Until now.

***

"My name is Victor Lang," he said.

The light caught the edge of his glasses, but not his eyes.

"I was twenty-one when we first did the play. Lighting tech. Part-time actor. All ambition, no talent. But I was... around her."

His voice went thin.

"Everyone was. Jasper. Clarissa. Theo watched her like she was the moon. And Harriet..."

He glanced across the room.

"You were just a kid. But you knew."

Harriet didn't speak.

***

Victor kept going.

"But me? She talked to me. Said she liked how quiet I was. Said I listened."

"I thought that meant something." He swallowed.

"The night she died, I went to the orchard because she asked me to meet her."

Everyone stiffened.

"She wanted to talk — to clear the air. She said she thought she'd hurt someone. Jasper, maybe. Or Clarissa. She wanted me to talk to them. To help smooth it over."

"I said yes. Because I wanted to matter to her."

***

His hands tightened into fists.

"Then she said she was leaving after the show. That it was just a summer for her. A memory. That none of this *meant* anything."

He looked up at Annabel.

"I wasn't angry. Not at first. Just... hollow. I begged her to stay. She laughed. Not cruel, just surprised."

"But that laugh—"

"It shattered something."

***

Simon spoke quietly. "What happened?"

Victor nodded. "I grabbed her. She turned. Pulled away. Slipped."

He blinked.

"She hit her head on the stone at the edge of the orchard. I panicked. Checked for breath. I could not find any. I froze."

"I don't remember carrying her. Just... covering her. With fabric from the costume tent. I buried her beneath the lilac tree. I thought no one would find her."

***

Harriet whispered, "You told me she left."

"Because you wouldn't stop asking."

"You cried. You followed me around. You knew something wasn't right. And I needed you to stop."

"So, I told you she left. That she'd said goodbye to me. And you... believed it."

She closed her eyes.

***

Annabel's voice was ice-wrapped steel.

"And Theo?"

"He saw something. Just a shadow. A glimpse of me dragging the fabric. He didn't even realize it meant anything — not then. But I saw the way he looked at me this summer. He remembered."

"I didn't hurt him. I just locked him away. I thought if I gave him time, he'd forget again."

***

Silence.

Even the fire seemed to burn more quietly now.

Simon stepped forward.

"Why come back at all?"

Victor looked at him.

"Because none of you ever left."

Chapter 25

The study was quiet again.

Victor had been taken to the sitting room. Harriet was resting. Annabel stood near the door, speaking in hushed tones to Evie, making plans to free Theo.

But Simon didn't move.

Not yet.

He sat in the chair where Victor had confessed and stared at the rug beneath his feet, worn at the edges. The same rug from twenty years ago. The same room. The same air.

And finally—after years of silence— he let himself feel it.

***

"I told her not to go."

He had.

He remembered it now. The way she'd smiled at him, always gentle, always with that little distance behind her eyes — like she'd already read your story and decided it was kind, but not hers.

"It's just a talk," she'd said.

"Victor is confused. He deserves a little clarity."

Simon had said: "Then don't go alone."

And she'd laughed.

"What could possibly happen?"

***

She had wanted to help. That was the unbearable part.

She'd never wanted to humiliate Victor. Or scold him. She had genuinely wanted to make things better.

He should have gone with her.

But he had let the moment pass.

And then Hannah was gone.

***

He'd lived in cities after that. Changed roles. Taught different courses. But Hannah stayed.

In the syllabi.

In the cast rosters.

In the space between acts.

He began collecting names.

Then contacts.

Then funds.

Not to write a play.

But to *re-stage a moment.*

To build the truth in *set pieces and monologues and lighting cues.*

***

"She mattered," he whispered aloud now.

Not just to him.

To all of them.

Even the ones who wanted to forget her.

But forgetting her was never an option.

Not after that night.

Not after that laugh.

"You deserved better," he said to the empty chair.

And then he stood.

It was time to find Theo.

Chapter 26

The prop shed creaked like it knew they were coming.

Annabel pushed open the door slowly, the scent of sawdust and age hitting her nose with theatrical precision. Simon followed, holding the rusted key Victor had reluctantly handed over.

Evie, flashlight in hand, swept the beam across the walls until it landed on a trapdoor beneath an old stack of painted backdrops.

"This was sealed up," Simon said. "We thought it was a coal store. I never imagined—"

He didn't finish the sentence.

***

Annabel lifted the latch. The metal groaned.

A narrow staircase spiralled downward, disappearing into dark stone.

"Stay here," she told Evie.

Evie nodded, jaw set. "Shout if you need me."

Annabel descended first; her breath tight in her throat. Simon followed; his steps careful. Dust curled in the air like forgotten dialogue.

***

The cellar was cold.

The air was thick with damp and quiet.

"Hello?" Annabel called.

Nothing.

Then—

A cough.

A scrape.

A voice, hoarse: "Hello?"

Theo.

***

They found him huddled on a thin mattress beside a broken wine rack, eyes bloodshot, a shallow cut on his cheek. He blinked up at the light.

"Am I dreaming?" he rasped.

Annabel dropped beside him, grabbing his hand.

"You're not."

Simon stood frozen; guilt laced through every line of his posture.

Theo blinked at him.

"You're the guy who ran the auditions."

Simon's voice cracked. "Yes. But that wasn't the role I came to play."

***

They helped him up.

He was weak, but standing.

Annabel offered him water. He drank like it hurt.

"I remembered too much," he whispered.

"I didn't mean to. I just... kept seeing her."

"You were right to remember," Annabel said.

He looked at her. And this time, the tears weren't from pain.

***

They climbed the stairs together.

Theo, rescued.

Victor, unmasked.

And Hannah?

Still gone.

But no longer forgotten.

Chapter 27

The lilac tree stood tall at the edge of the orchard, blooming late.

Its roots had held the secret for twenty years.

Now, they held nothing but air.

The earth had been disturbed quietly, respectfully. The police had taken what they needed. The coroner had confirmed it.

But this — today — was not for paperwork.

This was for Hannah.

***

They came in silence.

Annabel. Simon. Harriet. Theo.

Clarissa arrived in black, no makeup, eyes raw. Jasper stood beside her, holding a single script page, stained and folded too many times.

Evie brought wildflowers.

Persephone followed, tail high.

Even the villagers came, watching from a respectful distance — curious, but reverent.

***

Simon stood at the centre.

He cleared his throat once, then spoke without notes.

"We all knew her. Differently.

Some of us loved her.

Some envied her.

Some misunderstood her."

"But all of us... forgot the one thing that mattered most."

"Hannah was a person."

"Not a story. Not a performance. Not a ghost."

***

He stepped back.

Harriet came forward next, holding the violet scarf in shaking hands.

"She trusted me," she whispered.

"And I didn't protect her."

"But I see her now. I *remember* her.

I won't let her vanish again."

She placed the scarf at the base of the tree.

***

Annabel didn't speak.

She simply lit a small candle, set it beside the scarf, and closed her eyes.

Theo read a line from the play — the one Hannah never got to say.

"I will not fade.

I will not fall.

I am the line you forgot to finish."

***

The wind moved through the orchard
like applause.

No music. No bow. No curtain.

Just silence.

And peace.

For Hannah.

For all of them.

For now.

Epilogue

Rain tapped softly on the kitchen window, the kind that didn't insist on drama but arrived like punctuation after a too-long sentence.

Annabel stirred a pot of something aromatic. Evie leaned against the counter, nursing a mug of tea.

Persephone occupied her usual throne on the windowsill; tail wrapped around her like a feathered question mark.

***

"Feels quiet now," Evie said.

Annabel nodded. "Almost too quiet."

"Do you miss it?"

"The adrenaline?" Annabel glanced up. "Not particularly."

"No. The stage." Evie smiled. "The part we all played. Even the ones who didn't audition."

***

Annabel turned off the stove.

"I think we were all cast the moment that play was chosen."

She poured the stew into bowls, slid one to Evie. "Some of us didn't realise we'd been given lines."

***

Evie sipped her tea. "And you? What was your role?"

Annabel thought for a moment.

"I was the one who refused to improvise. The one who kept asking why the script didn't match the truth."

"Well," Evie said. "Every story needs a narrator with spine."

Persephone sneezed.

***

They ate in silence for a few minutes, the kind of silence that didn't demand filling.

Then Annabel spoke again.

"I think Hannah would've liked the ending."

Evie looked at her. "Even with all that came before?"

Annabel shrugged.

"She got the last word."

***

Persephone leapt down from the sill and padded over to the table. She pawed once at the envelope still sitting in the centre — Simon's last letter. Unopened.

Evie raised a brow. "Are you ever going to read it?"

"Not today," Annabel said, picking it up. "Some endings... can wait."

She slid it into the drawer.

The fire cracked in the hearth.

Outside, the rain washed the last of the summer from the leaves.

About the Author

Belinda writes layered mysteries where memory lingers, landscapes remember, and silence speaks louder than words. Her stories slip between the literary and the intimate—part atmospheric suspense, part quiet reckoning. Rooted in a love for islands, history, and hidden truths, her work invites readers to linger in the in-between.

She believes some lands carry echoes of everything they've witnessed—grief, joy, betrayal—and that nostalgia for a place is its own kind of story.

She also writes heartfelt children's stories that whisper courage into quiet hearts. With magical ladybugs, story-saving oaks, and brave little girls like Maia, Belinda hopes to help young readers find their own voice—and use it boldly.

When she's not writing, Belinda tends to her garden, guided by the rustle of leaves, the smell of earth, and the quiet company of two cats who always seem to know more than they let on.